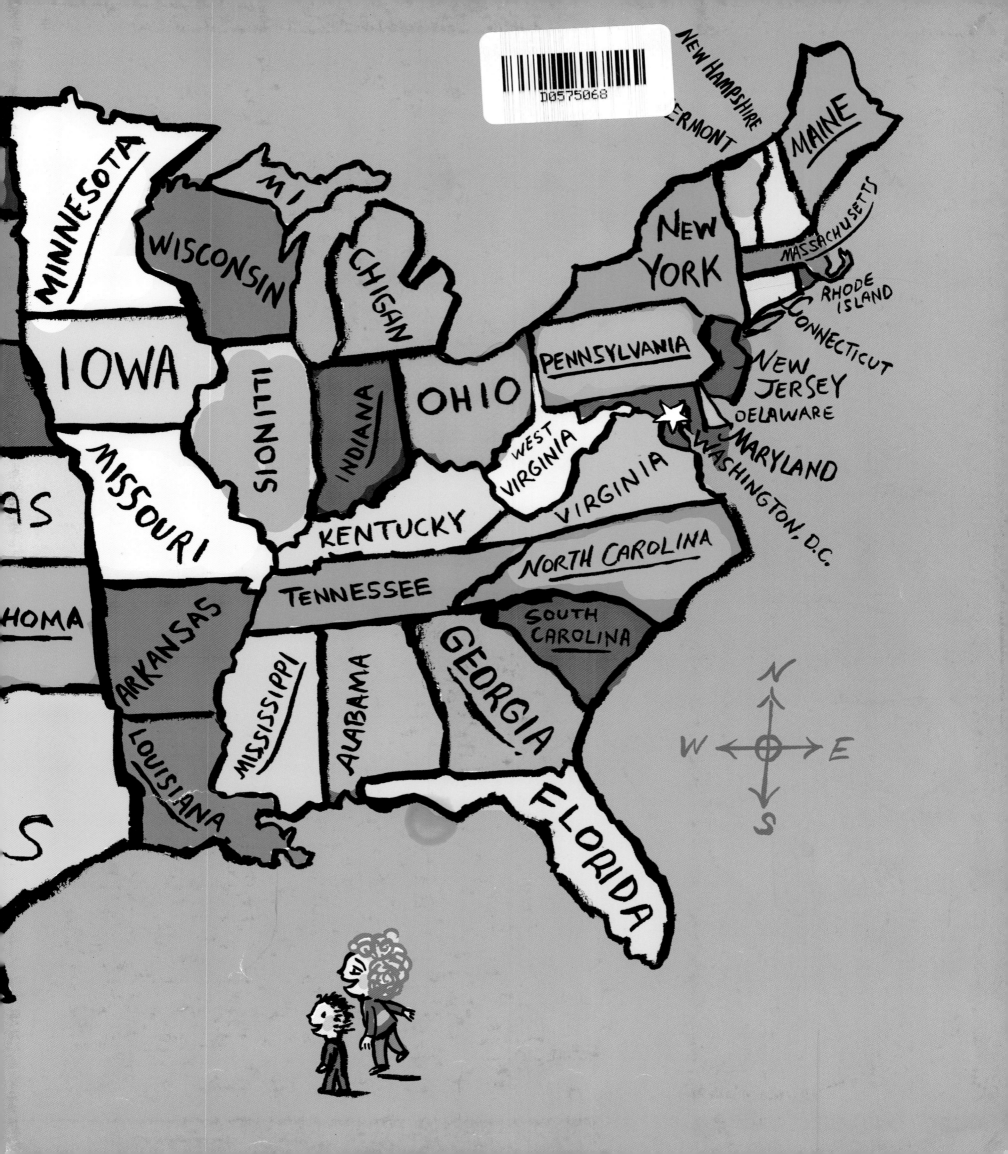

IZZY WAS A MOUNTAIN GIRL.... SHE LIVED UP ON TOP OF THE WORLD. IZZY'S LITTLE SISTER JO WENT RUNNING DOWN THE MOUNTAIN. SO...

IZZY FOLLOWED AFTER....

WOW!

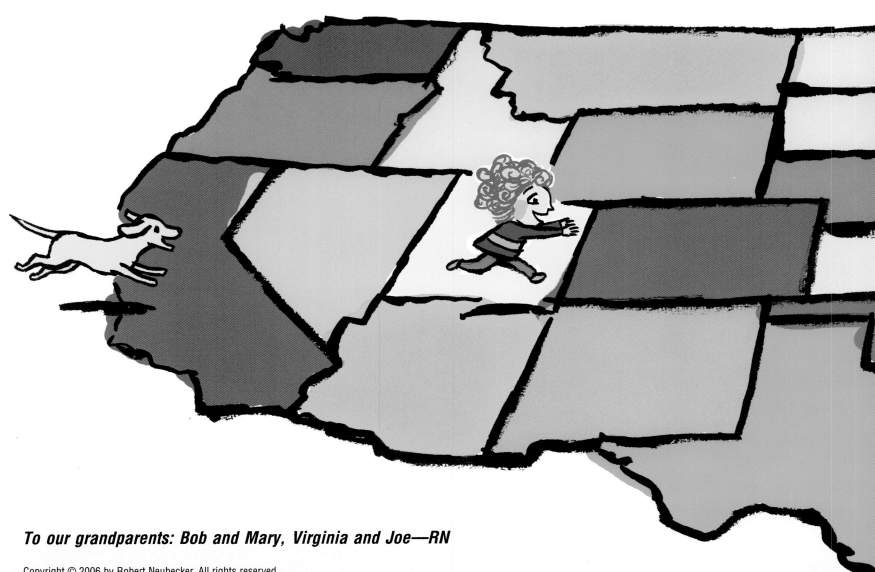

To our grandparents: Bob and Mary, Virginia and Joe—RN

Copyright © 2006 by Robert Neubecker. All rights reserved.

No part of this book may be reproduced or transmitted in any form or by any means, electronic or mechanical, including photo-copying, recording, or by any information storage and retrieval system, without written permission from the publisher. For information address Hyperion Books for Children, 114 Fifth Avenue, New York, New York 10011-5690.

First Edition

1 3 5 7 9 10 8 6 4 2

Printed in Singapore

Library of Congress Cataloging-in-Publication Data on file.

Reinforced binding

ISBN 0-7868-3816-7

Visit www.hyperionbooksforchildren.com

AMERICA!

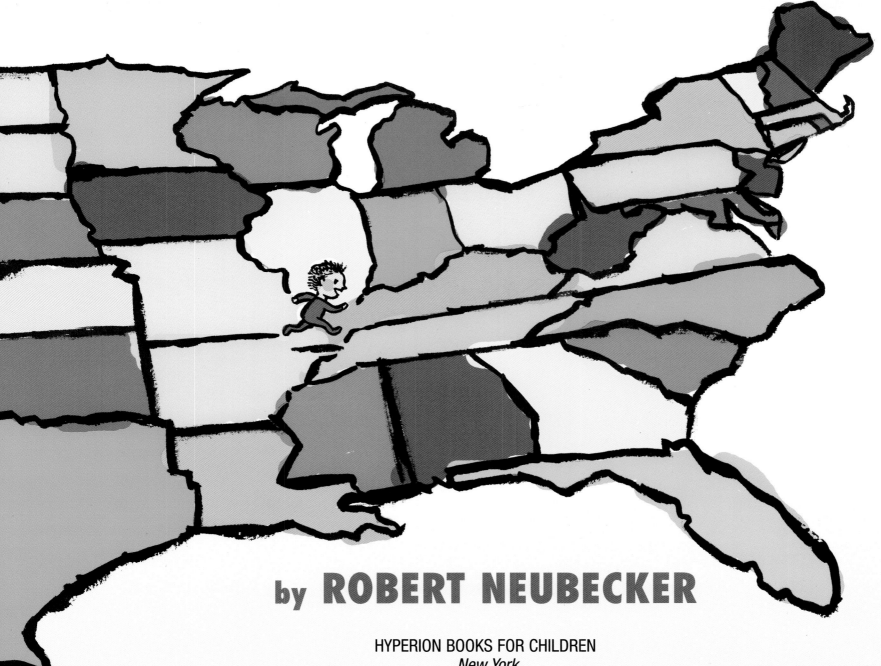

by ROBERT NEUBECKER

HYPERION BOOKS FOR CHILDREN
New York

STATUE!

CAPITOL!

SPACE!

AT CAPE CANAVERAL, FLORIDA, BIG

WOW!

WITH COSTUME PARTIES, MUSIC, DANCING—AND AMAZING PARADES!
JAZZ NIGHTLY

PARTY!

WOW!

WOW!

CORN!

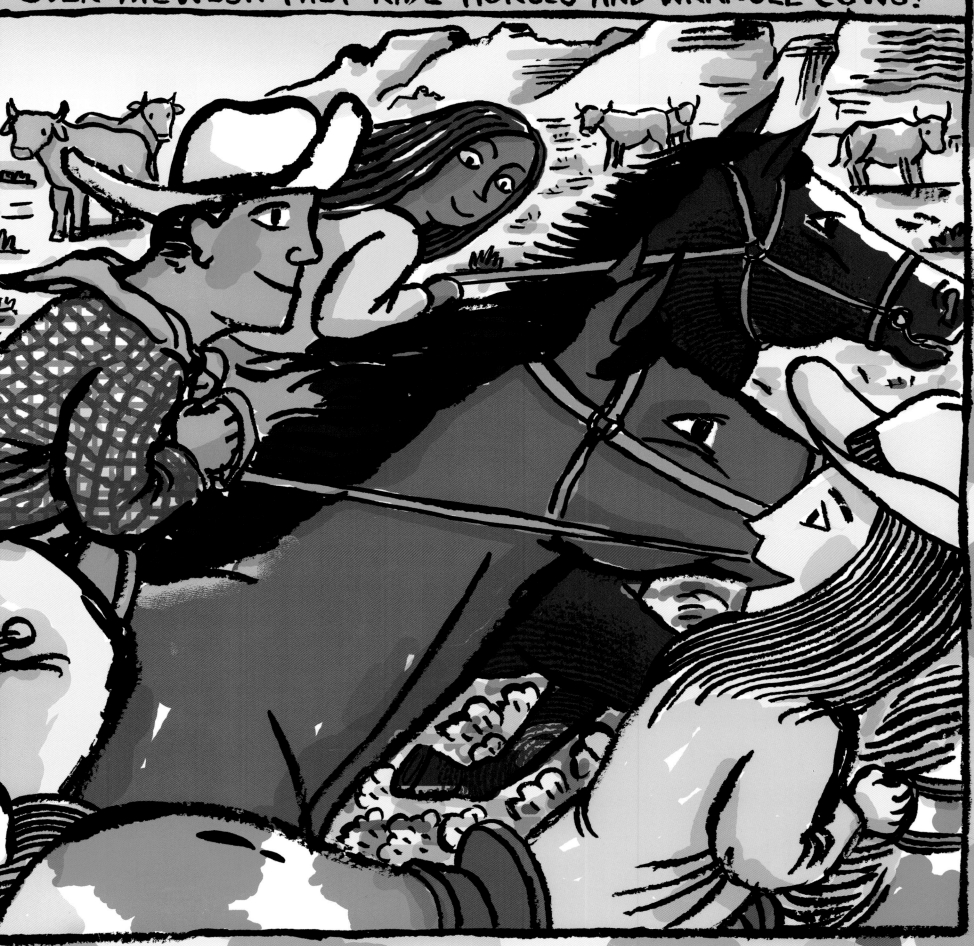

ARIZONA'S GRAND CANYON WAS CARVED

WOW!

MOUNTAINS!

WOW!

TREES!

GIANT SEQUOIAS IN CALIFORNIA CAN BE MORE

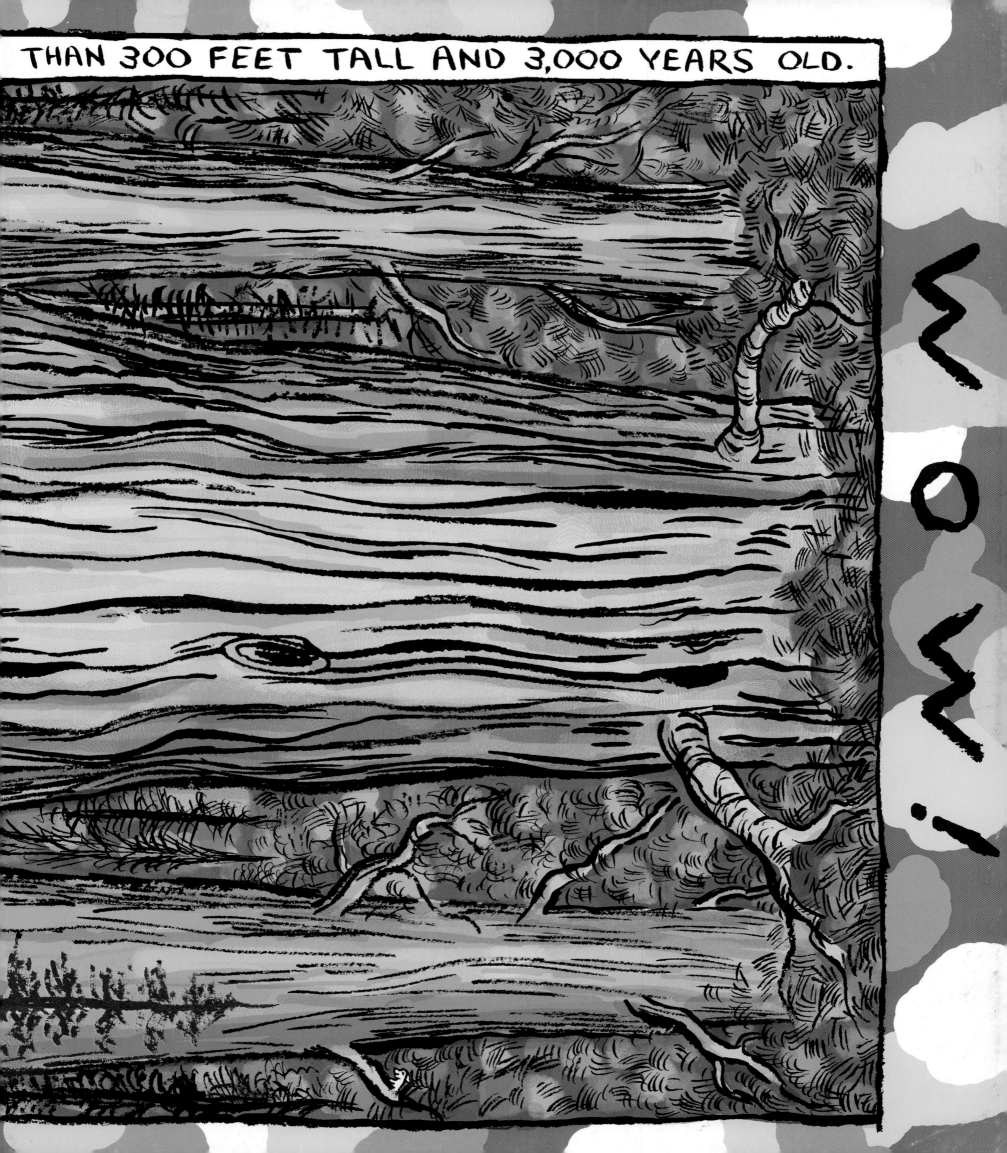

WOW!

MAUNA LOA IS THE WORLD'S BIGGEST VOLCANO.

WOW!

MOVING SNOW AND ICE THAT NEVER MELTS AWAY.

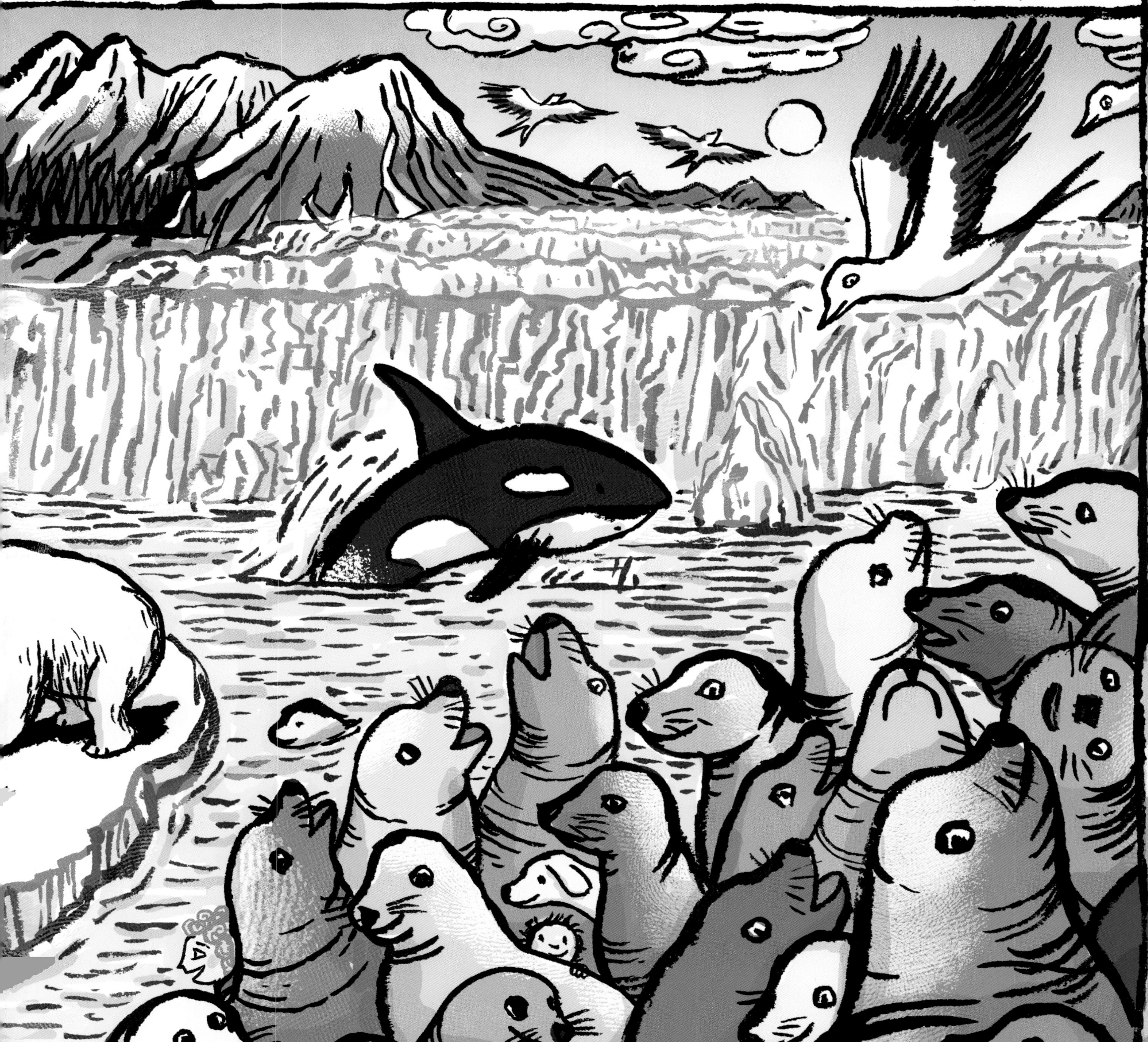

ICE!

WOW!

HOME!